THE PENGUINS' BIG WIN

written by Clare Mishica
pictures by Terri Steiger

STANDARD PUBLISHING

"Therefore encourage one another
and build each other up."

1 Thessalonians 5:11

The Standard Publishing Company, Cincinnati, Ohio
A division of Standex International Corporation
© 1994 by The Standard Publishing Company
All rights reserved.
Printed in the United States of America.
01 00 99 98 97 96 95 94   5 4 3 2 1

Library of Congress Catalog Card Number 93-36964
ISBN 0-7847-0139-3
Cataloging-in-Publication data available

Edited by Diane Stortz
Designed by Coleen Davis

CONTENTS

Ice Rink

Scoreboard

CLOCK   SCORE
2:42   HOME 3
VISITOR 2

Net

Goalie

Penalty Box

Blue Line

Bleachers

Players' Bench

Red Line

Center Ice

Players' Bench

Bleachers

Blue Line

Penalty Box

Goalie

Net

Hockey Player

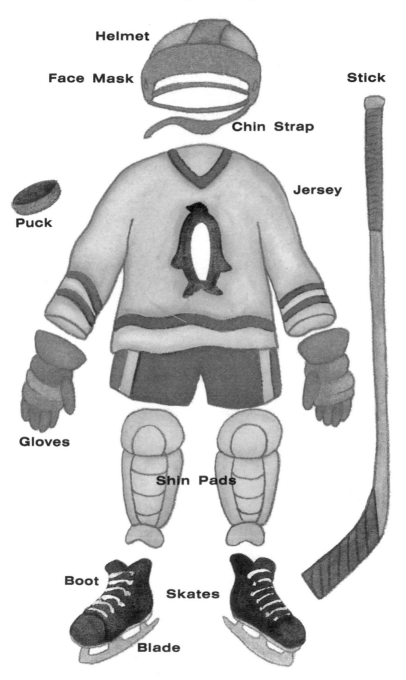

Helmet

Face Mask

Chin Strap

Stick

Puck

Jersey

Gloves

Shin Pads

Boot

Skates

Blade

Bzzzz! rang the buzzer.

"We are number one!"

cheered the Eagles.

The Penguins did not cheer.

They had lost

the hockey game.

"We will win next time,"

said Andy.

But at the next game,

Tami and Andy fell down

five times.

Carlos skated into the net.

Jamal and Kristen

lost their hockey sticks.

And Brian made a goal

for the other team.

The Penguins did not win.

"I know how to win,"
said Andy. "I have a plan."
"What is it?" asked Brian.
"What should we do?"

"Everyone should bring

something lucky

to the next game," said Andy.

"Then we will have good luck.

Then we will win."

Before the next game,

Brian put a lucky penny

in his skate.

Tami and Kristen

wore their lucky socks.

Jamal wore

his lucky jersey.

Carlos put

his lucky marble

in his pocket.

Andy wore

his lucky hat

under his helmet.

12

Bzzzz!

The game began.

Andy skated
onto the ice.

His lucky hat slipped down
over his eyes.

Andy skated right into Kristen.

Kristen fell down.

She dropped her hockey stick.

Jamal tripped over it.

Then Brian and Carlos

tripped over Jamal.

Andy's plan did not work.

The Penguins lost the game.

And they lost the next game,

and the next game.

"We will keep trying,"

Coach told the Penguins.

"We have

three games left."

"We will never win," said Andy.

"Kristen keeps dropping
her hockey stick."

"It is not me," said Kristen.

"Carlos skates into everyone."

17

"It is not me," said Carlos.

"Jamal gets too many penalties."

"It is not me," said Jamal.

"Brian shoots the puck

into the wrong net."

"It is not me," said Brian.

"Tami and Andy

cannot stand up."

"Stop!"

said Coach.

"We will not win this way.

But I have a plan.

Wait right here."

Coach's Plan

The Penguins waited for Coach.

"I can guess Coach's plan,"

said Andy.

"He will tell all of you

to pass me the puck

and let me score."

"No way," said Carlos.

"You would fall on the puck.

Coach will say

to pass it to me."

"Not you," said Tami.

"You would skate right over it."

21

Coach came back

with a hat in his hand.

There were papers in the hat.

"Is that our plan?" asked Andy.

"It is part of my plan,"

said Coach.

"I want each of you

to write a letter."

Brian scraped up

a pile of icy snow

with his skate blade.

"Who to?" he asked.

23

Coach held out his hat.
"Everyone pick a paper
from my hat," he said.
"Write a letter to the Penguin
whose name is on the paper."

Kristen skated a figure eight.

"What should we write about?"

she asked.

"Tell that person what he or she

does best," said Coach.

"Do we have to?" asked Carlos,

shooting a puck down the ice.

"Yes," said Coach.

"It is part of my plan.

Bring me the letters tomorrow."

The Penguins brought
their letters to Coach
the next day.
"Now tell us your plan
before the game starts,"
said Jamal.

Coach put his arm
on Jamal's shoulder.
"First I must read the letters,"
Coach said.
"Everyone sit down and listen."
"Do we have to?" asked Brian.
"Yes," said Coach.
"It is part of my plan."

Coach opened a letter.

"Dear Andy," he read,

"You can stop the puck good."

Andy smiled.

I will stop even better today,

he thought.

Then Coach read,

"Dear Kristen,

You pass the puck the very best."

Kristen put on her knee pads.

I will pass the puck

even better today, she thought.

The next letter said,

"Dear Brian,

You are good at putting the puck

into the net."

Brian tied up his skates.

I will put the puck

into the right net today,

he thought.

Then Coach read, "Dear Jamal,

You make good penalty shots."

I will make every shot today,

thought Jamal.

Then Coach read, "Dear Carlos,

You are a fast skater."

Carlos put on his helmet.

I will skate even faster today,

he thought.

The last letter said,

"Dear Tami,

You are a good goalie."

Tami picked up her hockey stick.

I will be the best goalie today,

she thought.

Bzzzz! The buzzer rang.

"Let's go!" said Coach.

"But what is the plan?"

said Brian.

"I will have to tell you later,"

said Coach.

The Penguins skated out

on the ice.

The Eagles skated out on the ice.

Bzzzz! rang the buzzer.

Swoosh! went the puck.

Kristen passed the puck to Carlos.

Carlos skated down the ice
very fast.

He passed the puck to Andy.

Andy skated near the net.

He stopped.

He passed the puck to Brian.

Brian shot the puck.

It went into the net!

"All right!" cheered the Penguins.

They had one goal.

The Penguins played better
than ever before.
Tami did not let the Eagles score.
The Penguins won the game
2 to 0.
The Penguins cheered.
"Good game!" said Coach.
He gave everyone a high five.

"I guess we do not need
to know your plan now,"
said Tami.

Coach smiled.

"But you do know it," he said.

"My plan is what the apostle Paul
wrote in the Bible," said Coach.
"Paul told people
to encourage one another
and build each other up."

"We encouraged

each other

with our letters!"

said Andy.

"Coach's plan worked!"

said Tami.

"You are the smartest coach!"

said Jamal.

"Yeah for Coach!"

cheered the Penquins,

and everyone hugged Coach.

"Thank you for encouraging *me*,"

Coach said.

"If we always encourage
each other," said Kristen,
"we will always be winners."
"Yes," said Carlos.
"Then we will be winners
even if we lose the game."